The Enclave

The Way to Freedom

Book 10

H.M. Clarke

Sentinel Publishing

Also by H.M. Clarke

The Way to Freedom Series
1: The Kalarthri
1.1: The Cavern of Sethi
2: The Dream Thief
3. The Awakening
4. The Enemy Within
5. The Unknown Queen
6. The Searchers
7. The Whisperer
8. The Deceiver
9. The Great Game
10. The Gathering
The Complete Season One–Books 1 5
The Complete Season Two–Books 6-10

Coming Soon
11. The Mark of Fate

The Blackwatch Chronicles
1: Proven

Coming Soon
2: Uprising

The Verge
1: The Enclave

Coming Soon
2: Citizen Erased

The Order
1: Winter's Magic
Marion: An 'Order' Short Story

John McCall Mysteries
1: Howling Vengeance

The Gathering

The Way to Freedom

Book 10

H.M. Clarke

Sentinel Publishing

Copyright © H. M. Clarke 2019

All rights reserved; no part of this publication may be reproduced or transmitted by any means, electronic, mechanical, photocopying or otherwise, without the prior permission of the copyright owner

First published in The United States of America in 2019

Sentinel Publishing, Dayton, Ohio

Cover design by Deranged Doctor Design

The moral right of the author has been asserted

DEDICATION

As always, this book is dedicated to my two beautiful children, Keith and Ariadne.

CONTENTS

Acknowledgments

Chapter One

Chapter Two

Chapter Three

Chapter Four

Chapter Five

Chapter Six

Chapter Seven

Chapter Eight

Chapter Nine

Others Books by H.M. Clarke

About the Author

"No act of kindness, however small, is ever wasted."

-A Saying of the Hater'le'margarten

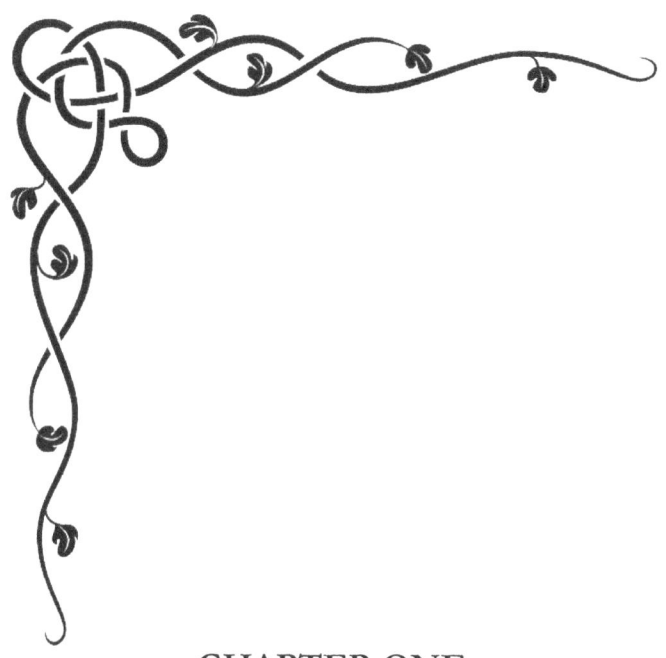

CHAPTER ONE

"There you are."

Dearen started at the sound of Tayme's voice when she, Hauga and Raga came through the door. When she looked up at him, he took a step away from her. It was then Dearen realized that her face mirrored the anger that she felt inside for

Asnar. She closed her eyes and took a long, deep breath, willing her facial muscles to relax. It took a few moments but once Dearen felt the tension ease from her face, she opened her eyes and forced a smile at Tayme.

"Yes, we're back. We've found Asnar. I don't think he'll be joining us again." Dearen gave Tayme an uncaring shrug of the shoulders.

"You didn't..." Tayme's half-finished question hung uncertainly in the air between them and Dearen saw Dalon Peana glance up at them from his vantage point across the room.

"He was still breathing when we left him-" Raga snorted, making Dearen stop and look up at him. "-Much to some people's displeasure." Dearen shook her head and moved to sit at the large table. "We didn't do him any harm," she said as

Tayme seated himself and his sour look in the chair across from her. "We asked him for the truth and he wouldn't give it to us, so we left it at that."

"Whose truth were you after?" Tayme asked. "Yours or his?"

Dearen glared at him. She could tell that he was upset, his flushed face made the purple birthmark stand out strong across his cheek. "Any truth would have been preferable."

'He still lied to us. And we were gullible enough to believe him.' Raga's voice cut into her mind. His anger will be with him for a very long time. The One, protect the next Pydarki that gets on his wrong side. Dearen turned to him and replied to him aloud so that Tayme would not be left out of half the conversation.

"I know he lied to us Raga. What's done is

done and we cannot change his, or our past actions. The only thing we can do is ensure we make the right decisions now with the information we have to hand." Dearen turned back to Tayme. "Which means that we need to get to the Dymarki Muster point and tell the Clan Council that we are on our own. Kral, I know you said that you and Trar were going to stay with me, but I will understand if you wish to go…"

"You don't get rid of us that easily Wing Commander." Tayme leaned on his elbows across the table. "My orders from Harada were to find you and keep you safe."

Dearen could feel eyes staring at them from across the room. "What say you Lieutenant Peana?" She asked staring at the man over Tayme's shoulder.

The Lieutenant shrugged. "The Hatar Kalar are not under my command. They have their orders."

"But what about you and your men though?"

"We still need to find our Captain. Our biggest lead is that he was going to come here, so here we will stay until we hear otherwise."

'Dalon Peana is worried. Capitan Vosloo is much loved by his men, and this disappearance is not like him. For some reason, the Lieutenant suspects foul play by the Pydarki.' Adhamh's voice slipped effortlessly into her mind and she accepted his presence because this felt…right.

'Really? Why is that?' she asked.

'Something that the Capitan had said to Peana before he disappeared. The Lieutenant has

the Tracker, Hanton, chasing up his Pydarki contacts to see if he can find out anything.'

'Which means that when we leave here, we will be leaving the Southerners- the Suenese – behind.'

'Yes. As Kral told you, the Hatar Kalar are coming with you. Harada and Samar, our flight Commanders, would flay the skin off Kral's back if he came back without you.'

'Really? Are they like that with all missing soldiers?'

'I don't know. You are the first Hatar Kalar to go missing in a Dragon's Age so I have no past history to judge this by.' Adhamh mentally sighed. *'All I can tell you is that you are important to Harada and others and that they will do anything to ensure you are safe…I will do anything to ensure*

you are safe. I say this not because of our Krytal link, but because you are like a sister to me, I have watched you grow into the person you are now and I want to see what you become. We are a team, a family and I plan never to leave you again.'

The conversation was taking an uncomfortable turn, even though Dearen felt a flood of gratitude for Adhamh's words wash over her. She turned her attention back to the man across the room.

"Very well Lieutenant. I wish you success in your hunt."

Dalon gave her a curt nod and went back to what he was doing.

"I take it you've already worked out what we are to do next then?" Tayme asked dragging her attention back to him.

Dearen leaned back in her chair. "Yes. We are going to join the other Dymarki at the Mustering grounds. We will then gather to meet the Northerners at Hatten's Field. How they greet us will determine what course of action we take from there."

"What about this renegade Arranian group? What if they try something? The information we have intimated that they are going to." Tayme shrugged and reached across the table to grab a handful of shelled nuts from a small bowl. Slouching back in his chair, he then used his thumb to quickly flick each piece into his mouth to eat.

The action caught Dearen off guard. Tayme had done it without thinking as he waited for her to answer…but seeing it now abruptly bought a vivid memory searing into her mind. They were both in someone's room. It was plain, utilitarian with a bed, desk littered with books, chair, trunk and a large brazier standing in the far corner. Her room from the feel of it. She was sitting on the bed dressed in the same black uniform that Tayme wore now. He was leaning against the small desk eating from a bowl. It was fruit balls this time and not nuts. She felt happy and he was smiling…

"Dearen? Did you hear me?"

She blinked rapidly, startled out of her memory. "Sorry? What?" Tayme was now leaning towards her, a puzzled frown marring his handsome features.

"I said did you hear me?"

"Ah…Yes…the rogue Arranians…" Dearen's voice trailed away as more memories popped into her head, triggered by the first. She was outside with Tayme and a blonde man, around them stood Adhamh, Trar and a blue Hatar called…Motta?

"Motta?" Tayme repeated.

Dearen's eyes widened. She hadn't realized that she'd said that aloud. But Tayme recognized the name.

"Motta's probably off nagging Holm about getting out of bed to come and pick ticks from beneath her wing pits or something-" Tayme's voice suddenly broke off as he now looked at her with shrewd eyes. "I've not told you about Holm or Motta and I don't think Adhamh or Trar have either."

"They haven't. I just…"

"Remembered them?"

"And you. I remembered you. Standing in

my room eating the fruit balls I swiped from the refectory kitchens…I remember doing that…" Dearen's voice dropped as the memory came again to her along with the taste of fruit balls on her tongue.

'Dearen, are you all right?' Hauga's voice slipped into her mind, worried but calm.

'I'm fine Hauga. I'm fine.'

"You were always taking the fruit balls. You like the taste of dried apricots, honey and sesame seed. Plus they were perfect to throw at Holm's head if you wanted to wake him up."

"Yes…And he would eat the balls afterward because he knew it revolted me," Dearen murmured as the memory formed in her mind.

"Yeah, I never cared much for that either. I slept in the same room with him for a while so I know how often he washes his hair."

"That would explain the smell then." The words automatically came to her and Dearen covered her mouth with the palm of her hand, shocked at how familiar that sounded.

'Dearen, how are you feeling? Are you okay? You shouldn't let Kral push you.' Adhamh's voice popped into her head and was filled with worry.

'He's not pushing me…I think I'm beginning to remember my past.'

'Dearen-'

Adhamh's voice was abruptly cut off as the muscles behind her ear began to violently twitch and Dearen thought she could feel something vibrating hard against her skull. She clamped both hands hard to the back of her head and squeezed her eyes shut as the pain began to lance through from her eyeballs to the base of her neck.

'Dearen?'

It was Hauga. She could feel his large, warm, gentle hand against her shoulder. But she couldn't move or reply. The vibration was growing, getting worse and now a loud buzzing grew like an echo in her ears. A mental cry of anguish cut through Dearen's head and she recognized it as Adhamh, now feeling the same pain as she. The only thing they had in common with each other was the crystals.

The Krytal Crystals.

Vague over her own pain, Dearen was aware of a new flood of mind voices, Trar, Hauga, Raga, Tayme's, all crashing and breaking around her like sea foam on a wave thrown against the rocks on the coast. The feeling in her head began to pulse in time with these voices, retreating and charging, until with one last tremendous rush it broke through the dark barriers at the back of her mind making them crumble and disappear like beach sand and freed what was trapped behind them.

A flood of memories spilled out from the breach and washed back to their homes in her mind, and her brain gagged on the torrent of information pouring into her. But out of all the images and voices flooding into her mind, she now knew one thing for sure. The Southerners had not been lying to her.

She is Kalena Tsarland, Hatar Kalarthri, and partner to Adhamhma'al'mearan.

But she is also Dearen of Clan Mufista,

Cearc of the Dymarki and sister to Hauga.

She remembered it all.

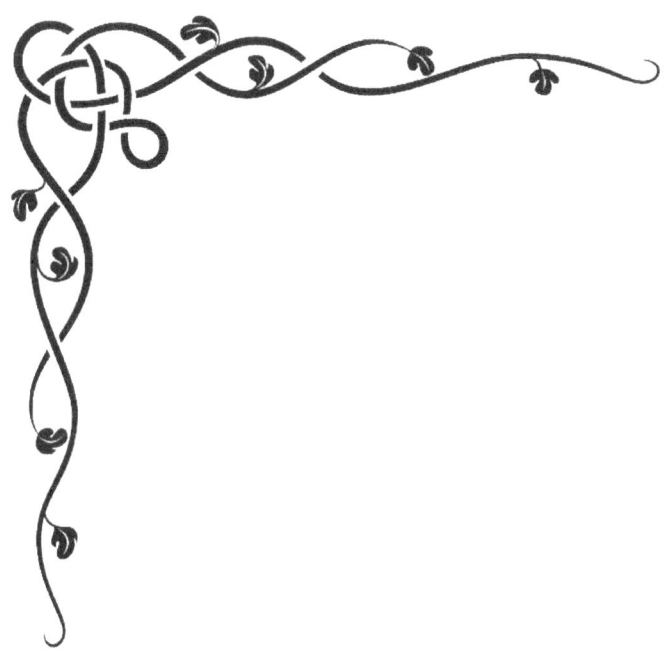

CHAPTER TWO

The pain and buzzing were suddenly gone. She pried open her eyelids and slowly released her head from her hands. Her body felt…normal. Her head was now filled with memories, from sitting in the tall trees along the steep cliff where she was born to growing up alongside Adhamh, Tayme, and

Trar at Darkon.

"Kalena, can you hear me? What's happening?"

Tayme was beside her, one hand rubbing her arm, the other brushing long locks of her hair away from her face. She turned and looked at him, but could still feel Hauga's warm hand resting gently on her shoulder. To her, they were the two aspects of her life, precariously balanced and still unsure how to treat the other.

'Hauga, the Southerners were telling the truth. I am Kalena. But I am also Dearen, and Dearen is who the Dymarki need now. Kalena will have to wait.'

'Dearen-'

'Did you hear me?' Kalena coldly cut him off.

A pause, then, *'Yes, Cearc.'*

Satisfied, Dearen then sort out another mind before talking to Tayme.

'Adhamh, are you okay? Something just happened to me and I heard you call out.'

Silence, and then, *'I'm fine. Now. The pain…it was excruciating. Like someone pouring boiling hot oil over every nerve and bone in my body. And then it was gone.'*

'I think it was our Krytal crystals. You say they are linked right? Well, now I know they are. I have my memory back and it was the Krytal crystals that got it back for me.'

'What do you mean?'

'My memories were locked away behind a barrier. The power from the Krytal freed them.'

*'You now remember who you were? You

now remember me?'

'Yes.'

Dearen could feel Adhamh's grin across the mental link and she now realized how much she had unknowingly missed him.

'So that would mean that whoever was powerful enough to knock us from the sky that day, also placed a barrier in your mind to make you forget who you are?'

'So it seems. And seeing as how Asnar has been lying to me since I awoke in that cave, I have a feeling that it was him and his secret group of cronies that were involved.'

'That would suggest that they were targeting you Kalena.'

Adhamh's words sunk hard and heavy into her mind.

'They were targeting us Adhamh. They knew that once they had me that they would have you as well.'

'Look at how predictable I must be.'

'You're a well know stickler for rules and are as loyal to the core to your friends Adhamh, you should not be surprised that someone would think you would want to save one of them?'

Adhamh did not reply but gave a mental nod.

'That then begs the question…what is so special about us?'

"Dearen!" The shaking on her shoulder grew more insistent and Dearen broke her connection to Adhamh to glare at Tayme's warm, tight grip on her shoulder.

"Are you okay? Trar is telling me not to

worry but-"

"Then you should listen to your Hatar," Dearen snapped. But then she relented when she saw the hurt that flashed across Tayme's face. She let her frown flow into a smile. "I was talking to Hauga and Adhamh. I can remember again. I remember who I was."

"Really?"

"Really." Dearen rose from her chair and threw her arms around Tayme's neck and pulled him to her in a tight bear hug. She felt his body stiffen in shock, then it slowly relaxed as he exhaled, his warm breath making the hair above her ear flutter.

"It's good to have you back Kalena." Tayme then abruptly pulled away from her to arm's length and looked at her shrewdly with brown eyes.

"But Adhamh said not to rush things. He specifically told Trar to remind me to keep my big mouth shut."

"Until I am ready to talk about it. And I am ready now." Dearen smiled at him again, trying to reassure him that everything was all right. At least, she hoped it looked like a smile.

It must have because Tayme smiled back at her and that silly grin was reflected in the rest of his face, especially his eyes. They sparkled when he was happy, yet another trait she now recognized.

"Please keep calling me Dearen. At least for the time being. It will make everyone's life easier if you do."

'Dearen, we have a visitor.'

Hauga's voice cut into Dearen's mind and she held up a hand to forestall Tayme's answer as she turned her head to look at the cat.

'What do you mean? There's no one here-'

Just as Dearen finished her thought, there was a soft tap at the door. Hauga flicked his black-tipped ears in smug satisfaction.

'You heard them didn't you?'

'And smell them. Some of the Pydarki do not wash their leathers. They need to let themselves run free more often.'

'I hope you're not saying they get naked are you?'

'By the Lord of the West Winds, No. I wouldn't curse that sight on anyone.' Hauga's light tone made Dearen relax the tightness she found between her shoulder blades. No matter what she had told Hauga earlier, she had been worried that her restored memories might change things between

them.

'You said Pydarki? I take it it's not Asnar then?'

Hauga gave her a single shake of his head. *'If he was out there, then Raga would be as well.'*

Speaking of Raga…

"Raga, you're closest to the door, please see who is there?"

'If I must.' The clan chief rose slowly from the table with what can only be described as a sour expression as his lips curled up in distaste showing his fangs to good effect.

'Dearen-'

'Shush Hauga. I trust Raga not to rip the throat out of every Pydarki he meets.'

'Except for Asnar.'

'Yes, expect for Asnar.'

Dalon Peana used a long finger to mark his spot in the book he was reading and sat up straighter in his reclined position on his bed as he watched the door.

Raga, his tufted ears pressed down firmly against his head, placed a large, furred hand on the door handle and opened it to reveal the young Pydarki again waiting in the corridor.

The young man's eyes widened at the sight of Raga's bared teeth, but the emotion was gone as soon as Dearen noticed it. The man's eyes then scanned the room, quickly coming to rest on her.

"I bring a message to Cearc Dearen from the Pydarki Council," he said quickly fishing a large folded piece of paper from a pouch on his belt and holding it up before him.

Dearen raised a hand and waved him forward and Raga stepped aside to allow the Pydarki to enter.

"I bring a message from the Council," he repeated as he stopped before her and bowed with the message held reverently before him.

"I thank you. I hope it bears good news."

A hiss from the door told Dearen that Raga did not believe so. *'You never know Raga, they may surprise you.'*

The Clan Chief snorted but remained silent.

Dearen smiled and took the message from the man. He immediately straightened and stepped away from her. The paper was heavyweight and looked well-made and was sealed with a large green wax seal with a stylized imprint of Daegarouf pressed into it. It was very official looking for a treaty denial. She could feel all eyes in the room watching her, waiting to see what the council's reply would be. Dearen ran her thumb under the paper's leading edge and cracked open the seal.

Opening the paper, she saw that it had been written in three different languages, two of which she did not recognize, in a very neat flowing script. Her eyes skipped down to what she recognized and Dearen began to read.

'Well?' Hauga asked after a moment's hesitation. Dearen knew that he was trying to preempt Raga's angry reaction.

"Just hold on, give me time to read it properly," Dearen replied without taking her eyes from the document. Her eyes slipped up to read the passage again and a spark of excitement began to ignite in her chest as her second read through confirmed that she had read it correctly the first time. She looked up at Hauga and grinned.

"By all that is holy!" Tayme was still standing close to her and could plainly read the paper she held.

"What is it?" Peana called from across the room.

'What does it say?' Hauga and Raga's voices echoed together in her head and Dearen had to stop herself from giggling. An unseemly thing for a Cearc to do in this type of situation. She cleared her throat.

"It seems that the Pydarki Council has decided to support us after all. They have pledged their warriors and Shamans in our fight against the Northerners."

Raga's ears jerked upright and his hackles

fluffed out in surprise. *'What?'*

'That is very good news.' Hauga's voice was laden with relief and she watched as his face relaxed back into the happy one she loved.

"There is a caveat though. The Pydarki will not do anything that would place their treaty with the Suene Empire in jeopardy. They are currently exempt from the Second Born Rule and do not want to do anything that would make the Empire enforce it."

'That is fair enough,' Hauga replied.

'We have no quarrel with the Southerners, as long as they leave us be,' was Raga's response.

"The Council would like to discuss troop numbers, logistics and what plans and strategies are already in place by the Dymarki." The soft voice of the Pydarki youngster seemed loud in the silence of the room, drawing all eyes to him. He had now straightened from his bow and looked expectantly at Dearen.

'I will go and speak to them Cearc,' Raga chimed in immediately. *'I am the senior Clan Leader and I have the most experience and knowledge of our Dymarki warriors and tactics. I also know our muster points and camps more intricately than you do.'*

'He has a point Dearen,' Hauga said. *'I have no love for politics and talk, if he wants to do it, let him.'*

"Very well Raga. You are now my War Chief. I am sure that none of the other Clan Leaders on the Elder Council will object. What say you Hauga?"

'There will be no objections. Raga is a

good choice,' Hauga replied enthusiastically. Dearen knew that he was just relieved that he did not have to bear the burden of War Chief on his shoulders.

"Then it is settled." Dearen turned back to the Pydarki. "I take it the Pydarki council want to start right away?"

The young man nodded.

"Very well. Raga, go with him and get things underway. Inform me of the details once they are hashed out, then we can get underway to join the others at the Muster grounds."

'Yes, Cearc.' As he spoke, Raga drew himself up to his full height, inclined his head and thumped his hand across his chest.

"War Chief." Dearen returned the salute and watched silently as Raga followed the Pydarki out of the room.

"Now that is a fine turn of events!" Tayme bust out as soon as the door closed behind them.

"Yes, I'm still a little bewildered by it all," Dearen replied as she sank back into her chair. She carefully refolded the Pydarki document and slipped it into one of her belt pouches. She would have to remember to give it to Otteren when they got back to CouncilMeet, the old cat would be ecstatic over having new lore to store in the Hall of Records.

Tayme slipped into the one beside her. "At least now you are not as alone as what you thought."

"I didn't think we were alone, not when I have you, Trar and Adhamh." Dearen smiled at him. "Kral, it is so good to have you back," she said leaning over and giving Tayme a hug.

"Kal-Dearen, you silly goose, I never left. But it is good to have you here again. I've missed my friend," he said as he returned her hug giving her a slight squeeze as he said 'my friend.'

'We need to start getting ourselves ready to go,' Hauga said as he walked around the table to stand behind her.

Dearen signed and pulled herself from Tayme's embrace, leaving a hand resting on his shoulder, reluctant to end the moment they just shared.

"You are right as usual Hauga. As soon as Raga and the Council have hashed out details, we need to be on the move to join our people."

'And we need to send an ambassador back to the Pydarki Council to ensure that they keep to what they have promised us.'

"Do you think it rash of me to suggest Drusa represent us as Ambassador? I know he is from our own clan and his choice might rub some fur the wrong way, but I trust him to look after our best interests."

'I think that's an excellent idea Dearen. And I don't think any of the other Clan Leaders would object. Mention it to Raga. If he has no issues with it then none of the others will have.'

"Thanks, Hauga." Dearen turned back to Tayme. "You may want to get all your stuff together. As soon as Raga gets back we are leaving."

"Thought as much. Luckily I don't have much. Just the clothes on my back, my trusty sword, and some saddlebags sadly in need of food."

"Food. Good point." Dearen turned back

to her brother. "Hauga, we will need to see if we can get provisions from the Pydarki before we go."

'I'll go arrange that now. That group we met earlier should still be in the common room. They'll be able to help with that.'

"Thanks, Hauga. I'll start packing our stuff. It's lucky that you, Raga and I travel light."

Hauga nodded and gave her a grin, flashing a glimpse of his front incisors before disappearing out the door.

"What do we do in the meantime?" Tayme asked as he reached across the table to grab the bowl of nuts.

"We wait."

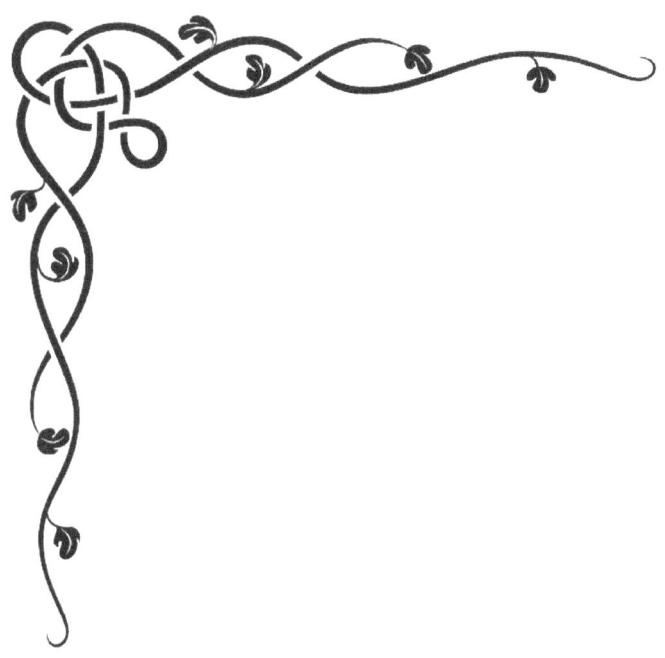

CHAPTER THREE

"Hanton, a word," Peana hissed at the lanky tracker as he closed his book over his finger to keep his place.

The tracker's head swiveled from watching the two Hatar Kalar to look at his Lieutenant as if making sure that it was Peana he had heard.

Peana frowned with annoyance and used his free hand to wave the man over to him. Hanton nodded and excusing himself from the other men, he rose from his chair. The movement reminded Peana of a stick insect rearing up to grab a higher branch and he quickly suppressed a grin before the Tracker could see it.

"Yes, Sir?" the man asked in a low voice as he reached the foot of the Lieutenant's bed.

Peana gestured to the bed next to his with the hand holding the book. "Take a seat, Hanton. We need to talk."

Hanton pursed his lips as he sat on the bed opposite the Lieutenant. As the man sat down, Peana swung his legs off the bed and leaned forward to face the Tracker.

"Have you heard anything back from your Pydarki contacts yet?" He asked, his voice hushed so that those at the main table could not hear.

The tracker shook his head, making some of his shaggy hair come loose from his pony tail. Without a thought, the man shoved the hair back behind his ears to keep it from covering his eyes. "Nothing as yet, but they assured me they will get back to me as soon as they heard anything."

"Do you believe they will?"

It was Hanton's turn to frown as if insulted by the question, but he nodded.

But Peana was not convinced. Before he disappeared, Captain Vosloo had given the impression that he distrusted the Pydarki and that they had something to do with Kalena's disappearance. The girl said that they didn't, but she couldn't remember anything from before she woke up with the Dymarki and she believes everything the Dymarki tell her. She may be their Leader, but a leader is only as good as the people they lead. And though the cats have done nothing against him or his men, Peana trusted them as much as he did the Pydarki.

"You need to go back to them and ask again. One of them somewhere, must know of or have seen traces of the Captain. By The One, the man said he was coming here."

Hanton heaved a sigh, shrugging his thin shoulders back as if he was uncomfortable about where this talk was going. "They will just give me the same answer Lieutenant. But I will do as you ask, I will find Jugar again but this time ask if they have seen or heard of anything or anyone unusual while patrolling their lands."

"You think we may have asked them the wrong question? What do you mean?"

Hanton pursed his lips again as if restraining them from spitting out the first thing on them. After a slight hesitation, he replied. "I had asked them if they had seen or heard of a Suenese Captain either in their lands or on Daegarouf. But what if the Captain did not want to be seen? You said he distrusted the Pydarki, maybe he's hiding out of sight somewhere watching them."

Peana's eyes suddenly lit up, "You may have a point there. A very good point."

"Either way, hiding or not, he would have left signs that someone had been around. One of the hunters would have seen them, maybe thinking they were Arranian."

"Good thinking Hanton. Yes, go and ask them that. And go now while the others are occupied."

The tracker gave him a curt nod and stood up from his seat on the bed. Peana couldn't help but think that the man should make a chirping sound like crickets do when they rub their back legs together whenever he moved. He tried to suppress the smile as he returned the nod and reclined back onto his bed with his book. He watched as Hanton said a few words to the men seated around the fireplace and then slipped out the door. The two Hatar at the table didn't even notice him leaving.

Peana's eyes lingered over the Hatar, more over Kalena than Tayme. He didn't know what to make of her and her lost memories. She was a Hatar Kalar, A Wing Commander, but now she was the Leader of these Dymarki Ice Tigers and she should be sympathetic towards the Suenese who are, after all, her people. That would mean that she could bring the Ice Tigers under the sway of the Empire. And he was the Highest Ranking officer here at this moment. A feat like that could bring him under the eyes of the Emperor, along with promotion, title, lands, and honors. Perhaps he should stay with them instead of waiting here in case the Captain showed up…

But as those thoughts floated to the top of Peana's conscience, his sense of honor and loyalty pushed them back down. They need to find Captain Vosloo. That is his number one priority. Taking one, last look at the Hatar, Peana then settled back more comfortably on his bed and continued reading his book.

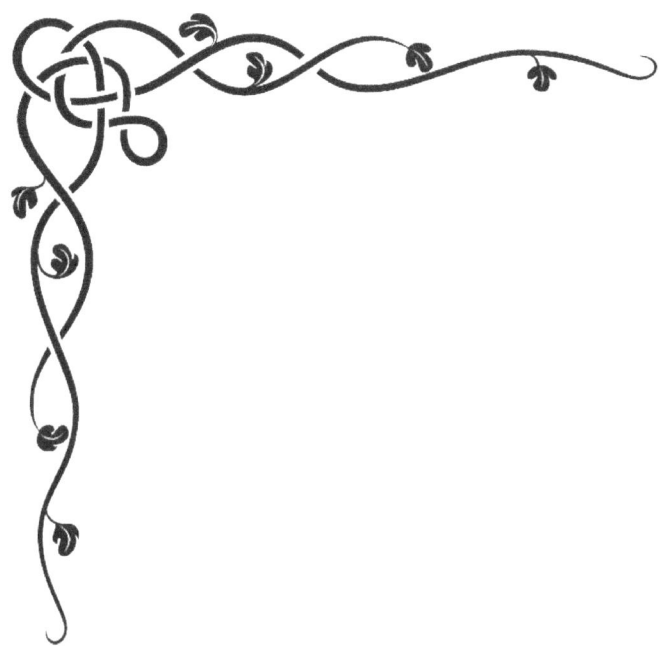

CHAPTER FOUR

'Hauga, can you hear me?' Dearen called to her brother again over the mind link but was met by only silence.

"Are you feeling well? You look like you're in pain."

Tayme's voice broke her concentration and

Dearen opened her eyes to see the Flyer sitting across from her with a worried look marring his handsome face. It was this new awareness that made her realize that she was frowning.

She smiled at him. "No. I'm fine. I was just trying to talk to Hauga, but I don't think he can hear me through all of this stone around us."

"Really? I wonder why? We can hear the Hatar perfectly well and they are housed in the thermal caves and from my understanding, there is a mass of solid rock between us and them."

"Maybe the Krytal Crystals help them somehow. Being linked with a pair of crystals may make talking easier with their partner. Or maybe the way they 'talk' is slightly different from the way Dymarki 'talk'. It doesn't matter how they do it at the moment because it still doesn't help me talk to

Hauga. I'll have to go and see what is taking him so long in the common room."

"What's so important?" Tayme asked. "I didn't think that I'd become as boring as Holm that you'd have to run away from me to shut me up."

"I need him to map out for me the quickest way to get to the Muster grounds, though since we will not have Lieutenant Peana and his men and horses with us, the four of us might fly there with the Hatar. It the Dymarki are willing."

"An Ice Tiger on a Hatar…The sight of that would be enough to scare the shit out of the Arranians!"

"Kral!"

"Awww, come on Kal-Dearen. That was funny."

"Well, yes, I suppose it is," she said with a

laugh as she pictured Raga clinging to Trar's back as she banked sharply to the left.

"Either way, I'm itching to be doing something. I can't stand all this sitting around and waiting, so I'm going to go and find out what is taking him so long."

"Okay. I'll write some reports for Harada. I'll leave them with the Lieutenant to be delivered back to Darkon."

They gave each other a nod and both rose from the table, Tayme to get his writing implements and Dearen to head for the door.

Once outside, Dearen leaned back against the closed door and sighed. That room was beginning to feel too enclosed for her tastes. Ever since getting the news of the Pydarki support, she now saw a smoother path going forward. A much better prospect than this morning when she thought the Dymarki would have to go it alone. The thought of leading the Dymarki into a losing battle had been gnawing at the back of her mind, and only now did she allow herself to acknowledge that they had a better chance of succeeding.

Huffing out a soothing breath, Dearen pushed herself away from the door and headed down the corridor in the direction of the common room. She had only gone a short way when she heard a noise behind her.

Dearen stopped and slowly turned, afraid that Asnar might take the opportunity of her being alone to try and get into her good books again. Instead, she saw a strange Pydarki.

He was very tall and his white hair was intricately braided and tinkled quietly with the small bells and charms that were woven into the braids. His skin was pale and wrinkled with age and the man's suede pants and tunic was the whitest she had ever seen on any Pydarki she had so far met. Since it was not dirty, he obviously did not do manual labor which meant that this man was either important or was too old to work, and since Pydarki do not see age as a limitation to work, that only left the first option.

"You are Dearen, the Dymarki Cearc?"

The man phrased it like a question, but to her ears, it did not sound like one. It sounded more a command. It put her on edge.

"Yes I am," she replied stiffly, unsure of what to make of this man. There was something about him that was familiar, but she could not quite put her finger on it.

"Please, come with me." The man immediately turned and started back down the corridor without looking back. He was expecting her to trot after him no doubt.

"What is this about? Are you a member of the Council?"

"I was. The Elders want to meet you before you leave."

The man answered without stopping and Dearen found herself being drawn after him. "The Elders? Weren't they on the council?"

The man shook his head causing the little bells to tinkle softly around him. "The Elders do not sit on the Council."

"So why do they wish to meet me? Is it because the Council ruled in my favor and they want to see me for themselves?"

"In a sense," was all he said.

They both walked in silence, moving deeper into corridors and areas that Dearen had not seen before, and seeing things that she thought could never be made by man.

Seeing her interest, the old Pydarki introduced himself as Angrave and explained that Daegarouf was built by the Ancients many centuries ago and for some reason, they had just left it. The Pydarki, who was the Chosen of the Ancients, moved into Daegarouf to keep the city safe for their return. The city was carved into the stone face of the mountain with walls and columns carved in intricate detail and depicted plants, animals and birds. Floors had been laid out in different colored stone to form complicated artistic patterns or outdoor scenes of rolling hills or orchards. Every corridor and room was lighted as if by sunlight from strange opaque bubbles in the ceiling.

"There is a hall more impressive," he said as Dearen asked if there were any more places that were grander than those she had seen.

"Is it on the way? We have been walking some distance and we still have not reached the Elders yet."

"Yes, the hall is just before the Elder's Chamber. They will not mind you to stop and see it."

They moved from the corridor they were in and began to follow halls and corridors and staircases that lead them deeper into the heart of the mountain. Dearen kept quiet and stared silently about her. They had seen no people since entering these deeper corridors but they showed not even a speck of dust. Dearen could feel the age of these halls as the two passed through them, they had the sense of having seen thousands of lives in their time. They also towered above them to heights of at least twenty feet and their footsteps echoed hollowly along their length. It felt as if they were the last two people alive on the mountain.

The thought made Dearen shiver.

Angrave kept walking straight ahead of her, not hesitating at any corner or junction. He knew the way but even Dearen could tell that the Pydarki was uneasy, as if ready to jump at the slightest hint or sign of someone else's presence. Perhaps the weight of the mountain above them made him unsettled. Dearen felt no such things as she could feel the refreshing drafts of fresh air being vented in from outside flowing through the Halls. These

Ancients certainly knew how to build.

Dearen watched as Angrave disappeared around a corner and nearly collided with him as she followed the man around it.

"What…" Dearen whispered before Angrave cut her off with a finger to his lips. The man then pointed towards the end of the corridor.

Dearen looked in the direction the finger pointed. The hall they had just entered towered higher above them than of any previously and ended in a T-junction. But what drew her attention was the sight of two huge golden doors that occupied the end of the hall. Upon them, styled in elaborate detail was curving trees and entwining ivy that looked to cover every inch of the doors. Set in the center of each door was the image of a rearing bison enameled in black with large glinting blue gems for eyes and steam rising from their nostrils.

Dearen stifled a gasp at the sight. It was the most beautiful thing she had ever seen.

"This is as far as I can take you." Angrave turned to her. "I am forbidden to enter the Hall."

Dearen was moving down the hallway before Angrave had finished speaking. She did not spare another thought for him. There was something behind that door, something that called to her. If she listened carefully Dearen could just hear it, as if it was miles away from her instead of just behind the door in front of her.

Before she realized it, Dearen was in front of the doors craning her head back to stare at the pair of huge black bison. Their blue gem-like eyes appeared to come alive. Their eyes began to whirl and seemed to shine with an inner light as if inviting her to open the doors. Then on the edge of her hearing, Dearen heard a mumble.

'I don't like this, I don't trust this man or this place,' Adhamh said but the sound of mumbling grew louder and quickly squashed him down.

The calling inside began to grow even louder; excited. The sound seemed to cascade through her mind giving her a feeling of ecstasy.

There was no handle visible so Dearen raised her hands to push the doors open.

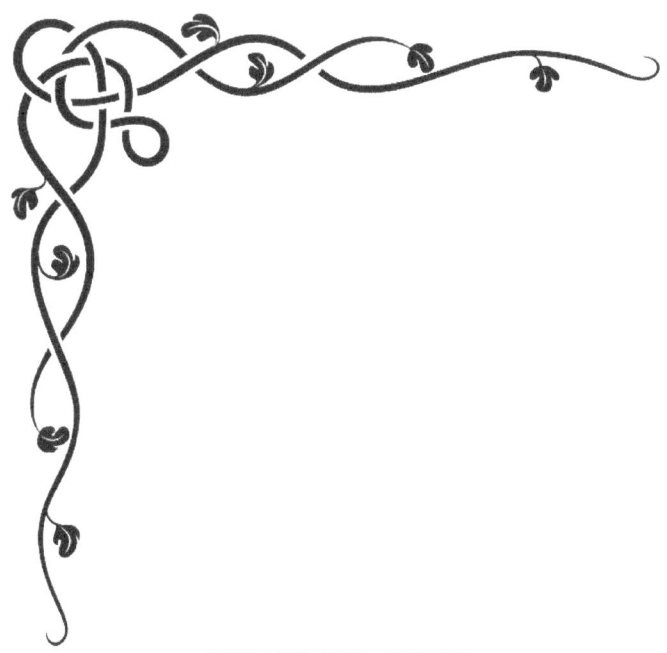

CHAPTER FIVE

Tayme looked up from his reports at the sound of the door opening. His smile dropped slightly as Hauga was the one who came through the door and closed it behind him.

"Where is Dearen?" Tayme asked before he realized that the Dymarki could not talk back to him.

The cat rolled his eyes in exasperation before quickly settling them into a frown as Tayme's words sunk in. He shrugged his furry shoulders and then jabbed a clawed finger at Tayme before jamming that claw hard against the table top.

Tayme's eyes widened in surprise. "I was supposed to keep her here? No one told me to do that!"

Hauga threw up his hands in indignation as if that was the most obvious thing in the world for the lowlander to know. Then the Dymarki's hands quickly flew into a blur of gestures that Tayme could not keep track of and definitely could not understand.

Tayme held up his hands. "Hauga, stop. I don't understand you. Talk to me through Trar, then I might have an idea about what is going on."

'Hauga is as testy as a cat dunked in water! What did you do to him? He's babbling nonsense and I can't understand him.' To Tayme, Trar's yawned question sounded as if she had just woken up.

"Hauga, you're going too fast. Trar can't understand you or your Dymarki swear words."

The expression on Hauga's face did not change but Trar sounded more awake and concise when she next spoke.

'Hauga is upset that you let Dearen hare off by herself.'

"But she told me that she was going to find you Hauga," Tayme said quickly in his own defense.

A few dramatic hand gestures with eyes

pointedly looking up at the ceiling and then centering on Tayme, Hauga replied.

'Hauga says that she obviously didn't find him. Why didn't she just call to him?'

"She did try and talk to you Hauga, but she couldn't contact you. She thought you were taking too long and wanted to go and rush you."

'She didn't make it to him down the hall,' Trar said.

'Can you or Adhamh find her and find out what's she's up to?'

'Give me a moment, I've got to wake Adhamh.'

It wasn't long before Tayme had Trar's worried voice back in his head. *'I can't hear her and I can't sense her anywhere in the mountain. Adhamh says she is here somewhere because he can feel her through their Krytal. He is going to try and search for her using that link.'*

'Is it just that she's not talking to you?'

'No, as I said, I can't sense her anywhere. Which means she is either out of range of our mind voices, or she is behind some type of shield.'

"She hasn't been gone long enough to be able to leave the mountain," Tayme said aloud. Hauga's ears pricked forward and he leaned on the table, waiting for the flyer's next words. "Which means she is either shielded from us by stone deep in the mountain or someone is hiding her from us."

'Hauga said that is his thoughts exactly and that Raga is on his way back from his meeting with the council. He wants to organize a search once Raga gets back.'

"Yes. The quicker we get started the

better," Tayme nodded at the cat. He then turned to Lieutenant Peana who was still reclining on his bed reading. "Lieutenant, will you allow your men to help us in a search?"

"For your Wing Commander?" The man said closing his book on a slim index finger to mark his page.

Tayme nodded and opened his mouth to explain but was cut off with a quick gesture from Peana.

"I heard, or rather, I got the gist of the conversation." Peana slowly swung his feet off the bed and sat up. "Yes, we'll help. My men can use this opportunity to ask or find out if anyone here has information on Captain Vosloo's whereabouts as well."

"But Lieut-"

Peana's voice cut straight across Tayme's reply and his teeth bit down on the rest of his words as the ingrained habits of a Kalar talking to a Freeman kicked in. Peana may not always be strict with protocol but it always pays to be careful when dealing with the Entitled.

"That is the condition for my help Wing Second Kral Tayme."

The Lieutenant's sudden formality reinforced Tayme's feeling, and he mutely nodded acceptance. They needed as many bodies as they could get to search a place this big.

'Hauga wants to start organizing the search parties now. The sooner it's done, the quicker they can start.'

"Let's start organizing now, Hauga says that Raga is on his way back so we can factor him in."

"Right." Lieutenant Peana placed his book carefully aside and rose from the bed to join the other two at the table.

CHAPTER SIX

The two huge golden doors stood silent as if absorbing all the ambient sound around them. Upon them, the curving trees and entwining ivy that covered every inch of the doors seemed to Dearen's eyes to move and shift as if being ruffled by a summer's breeze. The two rearing bison, enameled in black with large glinting blue gems for eyes seemed to stare down at Dearen and her raised hand as if silently questioning what she was doing. The stylized steam rising from their nostrils abruptly began to snort and their chests looked to heave with each exhalation. Their blue gem-like eyes whirled faster and shone brighter with an inner light as if now inviting her to open the doors. Then the mumbled voices that were on the edge of her hearing began to grow even louder; excited. The sound seemed to cascade through her mind giving her a feeling of belonging.

Dearen turned back to look at Angrave. The Pydarki still stood at the entrance to the hallway which in itself was wide enough for two Adhamh's to walk unhindered side by side. He was cloaked in shadows but there was light enough from the strange lamps for her to see him eagerly gesture her forward. His movements and the shadowed intense expression on the man's face suddenly made doubt rear its head in Dearen's mumble crowded mind, causing her logical mind to take control.

She turned back to the door, though door seemed such a poor word to describe this thing before her. It was larger and more impressive than the main gates at Darkon and in the larger imperial cities in the Empire. For something this large and ornate to be built, there must be something of great value inside to defend. Or to contain.

The murmuring grew louder as that thought entered her mind as if it was trying to reassure her. That it was no danger to anyone. That there was nothing to fear from it.

She turned back to look again at Angrave,

unsure now that she wanted to look in the hall.

"Maybe we should go and see the Elders first before I go in. If they want to see me, we shouldn't keep them waiting."

Angrave gestured again towards the door. "You have to go through the Hall of the Black Bison to see the elders. They are on the other side."

"The Hall of the Black Bison…" Dearen murmured to herself as she turned back to look at the doors. The same sounded familiar to her, but she could not remember hearing it before. "I've never seen a bison, much less a black one," she said aloud, more to bide time than any real interest in the animal.

"They were once numerous with herds stretching as far as the eye can see on the plains," Angrave said to her. "Bison were central to the survival of many peoples. They were food, clothing, shelter and they kept the plains clear of trees so that people could farm and their size deterred the large predators from the men of that time. Bison were also the primary prey of choice to the Dragons and the Hatar'le'margarten."

"Dragons and Hatar lived together?" Dearen asked, her curiosity piqued at the mention of the Hatar'le'margarten. Also, concentrating on the sound of Angrave's voice helped her to screen out the murmuring in her mind.

Angrave nodded and then continued his story. "Every Generation, the Bison would produce a pair with coats as black as pitch and larger than the smallest Hatar. These were sacred beasts revered by all as blessings given to them from the Earth. And through every generation they would live to old age and die on the plains, returning their sacred essence to the earth to be reborn again to the next generation.

"What happened to the bison? The herds are no longer with us, though I have heard that there are small herds of bison far to the North," Dearen asked without looking back at the Pydarki. She was watching the eyes of the bison. As Angrave spoke, the light in them seemed to slowly grow brighter. It may be a trick of the light, but Dearen was not so sure.

"They were hunted to near extinction here on the plains. A new group of people driven from their home by overcrowding came from across the Grotto Sea to settle this land. They greedily took nature's bounty and gave nothing back. Their towns and cities grew across the plains, taking from the bison open land that they once roamed, and the newcomers killed them indiscriminately, either storing their meat or leaving it to rot on the ground so that room could be made for more expansion. After several generations, the black bison decided to move what remained of their herds north, away from the avarice and greed of the newcomers. Then after that, the dragons disappeared and the Hatar'le'margarten had to find other prey to hunt."

"The newcomers were the ancestors of the Hadrians weren't they, my ancestors," Dearen said this more as a statement.

"Yes."

"Did the dragons follow the bison north?"

"No. They knew that their time had passed and they had made their own plans to help them survive and to help those generations in the future."

"What did they do?"

"That, I cannot tell you."

Dearen glanced sharply back at the Pydarki, not quite believing his words. His tone gave her the impression that the man knew damn well where the dragons had gone. But she was the guest here so she turned back to the door and did not push the issue.

"I've not heard that story before."

"As a lowlander, you wouldn't have. I do not think your ancestors even realized what had happened except that there was no longer any more easy meat. But we Pydarki and Dymarki did and we recorded the legend in the face of the door you now stand before."

"And what of the hall behind it?" Dearen asked.

"The Hall of the Black Bison keeps our legends and preserves our past. It is the heart of this land."

Dearen looked again at the door. There was no handle, no mechanism that she could see to open it. But the murmuring in her mind wanted her to open them.

She pressed her hands flat against both doors, expecting them to be cool to the touch as bronze should be, but instead she felt the metal was warm. As soon as her skin touched the metal, heat pricked across her senses and flowed effortlessly from the door into her hands and arms, quickly filling them and pushing away the cold of the surrounding mountain stone from her bones and skin. The heat then flowed up her neck and began to tickle at the scar behind her ear. At the scar left behind by the Krytal.

A loud creak resounded through the corridor and the metal behind her hands began to vibrate. And then move.

Dearen jerked her hands away and jumped back, surprised, as the giant doors slowly opened inwards by themselves.

Beyond the doors, Dearen saw a huge space open up before her. But the room beyond was not dark. The doors revealed walls that flashed and glittered in a multifaceted play of light as every inch of their surface was covered in varying sizes of pink crystal forms that each produced their own inner light. Painful memories of Sethi'de'hasma rose in her mind as Dearen noted the cosmetic similarities between this Hall and the hidden cavern at Darkon.

Whispers of many voices teased at the edge

of her hearing, their sibilant sounds calling to her to come in and talk to them. Dearen stepped forward and the voices instantly fell silent.

She looked back again at Angrave who motioned again for her to go through the doors. Dearen hesitated. She did not really feel threatened by the Hall, or the crystal, or her memories of what happened the last time she entered a crystal room, but Dearen still felt uneasy. Maybe it was Adhamh's warning still echoing in her head.

The voices began to whisper again and this time, Dearen felt an answering tingle in the back of her mind answering their call and working to impel her to walk past the doors. It was her Krytal. She didn't know how she knew that, but she was certain of it. A faint tugging told her that the Krytal link with Adhamh was also active. Whatever was calling to her was calling to him as well.

Dearen turned away from Angrave and looked back into the Crystal hall behind the ornate doors. There was only one way to find out what was going on.

She took a deep breath to steel herself and stepped through the doors.

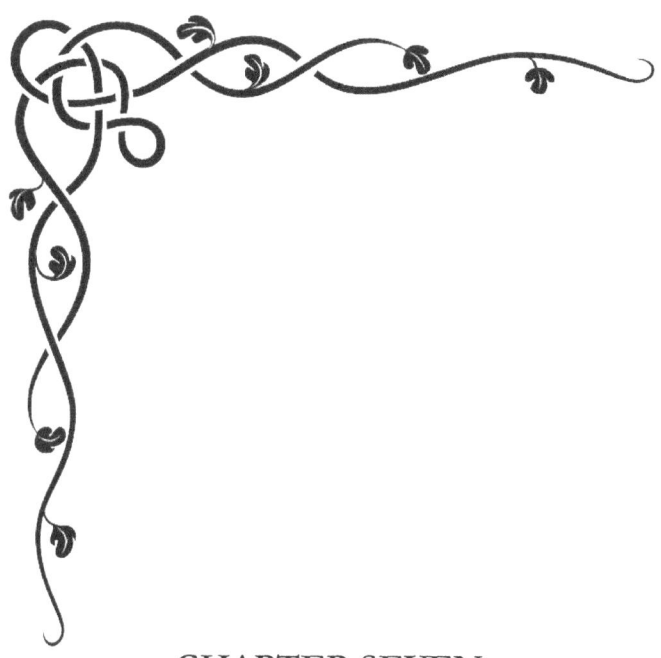

CHAPTER SEVEN

By the One, where is she?

There was no sign of Kalena-Dearen anywhere. Tayme winced as he corrected the name in his mind. She wanted to be called Dearen and Dearen it shall be. Now if only his subconscious will let him do it.

He and Hauga had searched more rooms, halls, and corridors than he could count. And judging from the set of the big cat's shoulders, he was just as frustrated as Tayme. Hauga's signed gestures were stiff and jerky and Tayme made sure to stand outside of the cat's reach in case the Dymarki wanted to hit something with his tree trunk arms.

'Trar, ask Hauga where he thinks we should search next.'

'Yes, Kral. I warn you, I don't think he's in much of a good mood at the moment.'

'I gathered that Trar. I'm not in that fine a one myself.' On those words, Tayme mentally took charge of himself. It would not do to let the worry or the dread he felt rising up from the pit of his stomach to overwhelm him. He had lost her once;

he was not going to let it happen again.

'We'll find her Trar.'

'I know. I'll ask Hauga where he wants to go next.'

Trar was only gone a few moments before she was back in his mind. *'Hauga's just had word from Raga.'* At the same time, Hauga had turned to him and started excitedly gesticulating.

'He's found her?'

'No. Not that. Raga has found Asnar. He is taking him back to our room. Raga thinks that he knows where Dearen is.'

'Does he now…'

Tayme smiled grimly and looked up at Hauga.

"Trar just told me Raga has Asnar, and that he thinks Asnar knows where Dearen is."

Hauga nodded, gave a few brief gestures along with a snarl and started back down the corridor, leaving Tayme staring after him.

'He's heading back, he wants to be there when Raga drags him in,' Trar told him.

'Okay.' Tayme replied to Trar before scurrying to catch up with Hauga.

"Do you really think Asnar would do something to Dearen?" He asked Hauga as he fell in beside the big cat.

Hauga made a few gestures with his hands along with some threatening grunts while he continued his quick pace through the hallways.

'He says that he wouldn't put anything past that Ajunti. After they found out the Pydarki lied to the entire Dymarki people whose to say what he wouldn't do,' Trar relayed to Tayme without much

enthusiasm. The Hatar did not agree with Hauga.

"How would that help him though?" Tayme asked Hauga. "I can't see what he could gain from her disappearance? After all, the council is now supporting the Dymarki which is what he wanted isn't it?"

'Who can say what that fool thinks or really wanted. If Raga says he had something to do with Dearen's disappearance then I believe him.' Trar's voice was monotone, something Tayme was not used to hearing from her.

'Trar, are you okay?' He asked the Hatar in concern.

'Yes, I'm fine. It's just Hauga's thoughts are not very coherent. He cares about Kalena very much and he is slowly building himself up to do something he might regret later. He won't listen to

me though.'

'He's not going to be listening to me either Trar. The only human he will listen to is the one who is now missing.'

'Just be sure that nothing untoward happens to Asnar when Raga gets him back. He may not be well liked here but he is still a Pydarki. You never know how they are going to react if something happens to one of their own.'

'I know Trar. I know.'

After that, they walked together in silence with only a cursory nod given to any Pydarki they passed. Tayme used the time to furiously think of ways to divert any Dymarki 'excess' used in any 'talk' with Asnar. If the man *did* have anything to do with Dearen's disappearance then Tayme would be the first in line to get answers. But until they knew that for sure, he will need to make sure that Hauga did not do anything that he might later regret.

As they approached the door to their room Tayme could hear the sounds of raised male voices mixing with the agitated snarls of a Dymarki. He glanced at Hauga and without a word, they both sprinted to the door and Tayme flung it open to let the big cat storm through. Hauga was the only one here that could physically hold Raga back from doing something stupid.

Before Tayme could shut the door behind them, Hauga had reached out to grab Raga by the shoulders and pulled him back into a nearby wall. A disheveled Asnar was standing not that far away from him and between Raga and the Pydarki stood Lieutenant Peana, his arms still raised out like a bulwark between them.

Raga was bigger than Hauga but did not inhibit Hauga from neatly pinning him to the wall and grabbing Raga's attention enough to calm him a little. Asnar looked no better. His face was red with fury and with his hair and clothes in disarray, looked more like a raging harridan than an ascetic Pydarki. Tayme tried not to laugh at the comparison, he shouldn't be insulting old women like that.

A slight nod from Hauga told Tayme that the Dymarki had Raga under control and so he moved his attention solely on the irate Pydarki who was now yelling at Peana.

"-LET ME OUT. YOU'VE NO RIGHT TO KEEP ME HERE."

"Just calm down. We cannot sort this out

until you have both calmed down," Peana replied to him, his voice measured and even and reminded Tayme of a trainer talking to a skittish animal. Once Asnar had stopped his yelling and Raga his snarling, Tayme stepped forward and pulled a chair out from the table.

"Asnar, sit down. We need to talk." Tayme patted the top of the chair as he spoke, getting a raised eyebrow from the Lieutenant. The expression so mirrored one of Dearen's that Tayme had to forcefully stop himself from sniggering.

After all that shouting, the Pydarki now stood looking at him through narrowed eyelids as if sizing him up. Asnar was a big man, Tayme would give him that. But just because Tayme looked slight didn't mean he couldn't hit hard. The Hatar Kalar stared calmly back at him, daring the man to try something. They both stood staring at each other as if competing in a silent battle of wills until the spell was broken by a loud snort from Raga.

'Raga says to stop pissing around and make him talk.' Trar said with a touch of distaste. Tayme knew that she wasn't one for vulgar language. *'Adhamh is acting strangely. He says that there is something happening with Kalena, though he can't pin point where. He also says that his connection with Kalena flashes on and then disappears again but it is not enough for him to locate her.'*

'Is he saying that something or someone is blocking her?'

'Maybe. He doesn't say that outright, what he does say doesn't make much sense.'

'What exactly is he saying Trar?'

'Well-' There was a pause as Trar's presence

in Tayme's mind retreated. Within a heartbeat, she was back. *'He says that it feels like the block is coming from her or something near her.'*

'What? That's what he thinks? You're right; he's not making much sense.'

"Wing Second?"

'Keep me updated Trar.'

'Yes, Kral.'

Tayme's ears focused on Lieutenant Peana voice, but his eyes were still staring at Asnar who was standing as still as stone.

"Asnar, I suggest you sit," he said tapping the back of the chair again.

After another moment's hesitation, Asnar slowly moved to sit stiffly down on Tayme's chair. He then sat like a stone statue, staring out across the wooden table to the fireplace as if he was waiting for someone.

"Did Raga tell you why he bought you here?" Tayme began, still standing behind the chair just outside of Asnar's field of view. When the Pydarki did not answer the Flyer continued. "Dearen has disappeared. We've no idea where she is or who could have taken her." Tayme leaned forward and gripped the back of the chair. The Pydarki still did not move. "This has me worried, and our Dymarki friends are very eager to get her back by any means necessary. Very eager."

"How do you know someone has taken her? She may just be lost. Daegarouf is a big place." Asnar's voice was soft and even, a complete opposite to his shouting earlier. *Something has steadied him.*

'You have something there Kral,' Trar's

voice slipped easily into his mind. She had been listening in to his thoughts and conversations.

'Why?'

'Adhamh's been focusing on him since he is our only tangible lead at the moment. And he felt something pass between Asnar and someone else.'

'You mean he's in contact with someone?'

'Adhamh seems to think so. He could not hear the exchange though. The link is shielded.'

'Trar, tell Hauga. He may have better luck with cracking a Pydarki's thought shields.'

'Yes, Kral.'

"Kal- Dearen would never wander off by herself. Not without telling someone what she was doing." Not strictly true but Asnar did not need to know that Tayme reasoned. From the corner of his eye, Tayme saw Hauga's reaction to Trar's message. And then a heated look passed between Hauga and Raga before Hauga released his grip from Raga's shoulders.

Asnar's head suddenly whipped round to stare at the Dymarki and Tayme saw Raga take a step forward. Raga must have said something.

'I'd back away if I were you, Kral.'

Trar's urgent warning automatically jerked him back a few steps from the chair. Asnar must have noticed the movement as he glanced at Tayme before quickly focusing back on Raga.

'What's going on Trar?'

'The four of us have planned something.'

'Four?'

'Adhamh and me and the Dymarki. Just guard the door and watch.'

Tayme stared at both Raga and Asnar,

trying to keep both in his field of vision. Not a word or sound came from either of them, but something was clearly happening as the expression on Asnar's face changed from a calmness set in stone to a mix of consternation and surprise, Tayme couldn't decide which. Then Asnar took a step forward as if he wanted to go toe to toe with the big cat and Raga started to lean out from the wall, daring him to. Tayme was about to move to pull the man back but Trar stopped him.

'Don't.'

'But Raga could tear him to pieces!'

'Just watch.'

'How is this going to help us find Kalena?'

'Just watch and be patient.'

The two stood facing each other, angry, bristling and aggressive. But, apart from that first step they did not move. Hauga was staring Asnar down, but not threatening. The two were obviously talking together.

Then Ansar's head jerked and turned away from the Dymarki. He closed his eyes and frowned as if in pain and after a sigh and a deep breath, Asnar turned to Tayme.

"I know where she is. I will lead you to her."

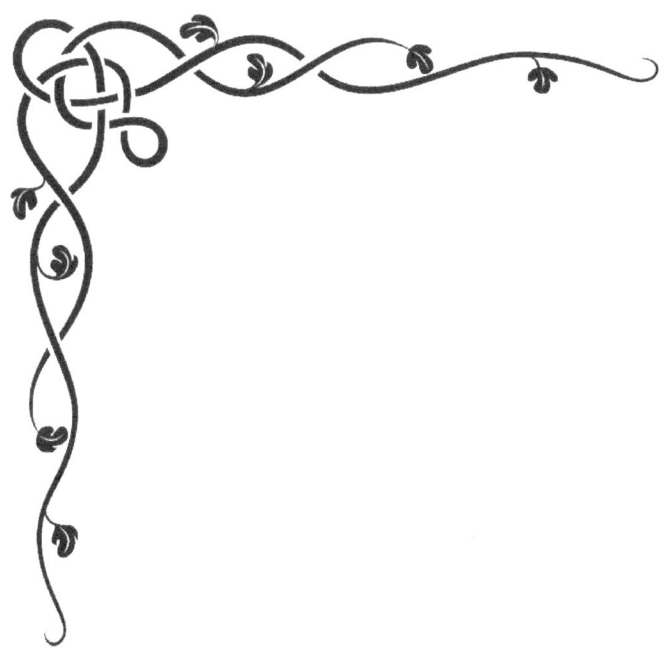

CHAPTER EIGHT

"What have you done to her?"

Tayme leapt before he had finished speaking and it was only Raga's speed and dexterity that stopped him from doing harm to the Pydarki. Lieutenant Peana moved behind Asnar, ready to hold him if he tried to engage with Tayme.

"Raga, let me go!" he cried, straining hard against the Dymarki's hold on his shoulders.

'Kral, calm down,' Trar's voice slipped into his mind and it was her steadiness that helped to settle him.

'He knew all along where she was!'

'No he didn't,' Trar replied. *'But he's been in communication with the one who has her. Adhamh heard them talk before Asnar spoke. Asnar seemed just as surprised as you are.'*

'What?' Tayme asked as confusion flooded through him, making him relax enough for Raga to risk releasing him from the tight hold.

'Asnar had mentioned to Hauga and Raga that he had been working with a group. We surmised that it might have been someone from this group that has Kalena. We decided that if we put

Asnar under enough stress that he might try to contact someone to see what was going on. And he did and got an answer.'

'*Does Adhamh know who?'*

'*No names were mentioned, but Adhamh said that there was something about the voice that was familiar.'*

'*Okay Trar, tell Raga that I'm fine, he doesn't need to stand over me like that.'* Tayme looked up into the big cat's face and after a few moments, Raga stepped away from him though his ears still stayed flat against his head.

'*What was Asnar told then?'*

'*Basically, he was told to bring us to something called The Hall of the Black Bison. That is where Kalena is.'*

'*Is that here in Daegarouf?'*

"I know where she is and I'll take you all to her. The leader of my group has her and that is all I can say." Asnar's voice broke the silence of the room. Hauga turned to Asnar and after a moment Asnar visibly stiffened. "No need to remind me that I cannot run, that a Dymarki can chase me down no matter what shape I choose."

'Trar, what was that about?'

'Hauga gave a warning not to run which seemed to upset Asnar. I didn't understand it much, it made no sense to me.'

'It doesn't matter. Whatever it takes to bring Kalena back.'

"Lead us to her Asnar. And I'll add my threat to the one Hauga just gave you. If anything has happened to her then you will have to deal with Trar and me."

"There is no need for all the threats. Dearen will be fine. She is not being held against her will, she went of her own accord."

Raga made a sharp gesture that needed no translation from Trar.

"We will ask Dearen ourselves when we find her Asnar," Tayme shot off the comment automatically. Something about the Pydarki rubbed him the wrong way. Lieutenant Peana obviously felt the same way from the expression on his face. The man was looking at Asnar as if he was a cockroach that had escaped being stomped by his booted foot.

"You all go. I'll wait here for my men to return," Peana said, though he still stood behind Asnar as if he thought the Pydarki might try to escape the room.

Hauga reached out and caught Asnar by the arm and propelled him towards Tayme and the door. Peana jumped back in surprise and Tayme sidestepped to get out of their way. Raga moved quickly to get the door and then before Tayme was really aware of what was going on, they were all in the corridor quick marching as fast as they dared to Asnar directions.

'Trar, ask Raga if we can really trust this man. For all we know he could be leading us all to our doom. To be lost forever in Daegarouf's endless tunnels.'

In what seems like moments, she answered him back.

'Raga says that Asnar wouldn't dare do that. It's worth his life not to.'

'I just don't want to get lost in these

hallways Trar.'

'The Dymarki will be able to find their way back Kral. Just stick with them and you will bring Kalena back home.'

'If you say so.'

Tayme stopped conversing after that and just concentrated on keeping track of the path they took. It would have salved his worry more if he knew that they were taking the same course that Kalena had taken not long before them. The group moved quickly through the corridors though Tayme, unlike Kalena, did not have the luxury of looking at the architectural splendors on display around them.

Then suddenly Trar was in his mind again.

'There is something wrong with Adhamh. There was a flash of pink light and he just went rock still. He then started calling out incoherently to

Kalena.'

'I thought he couldn't detect her? Can he feel her now?'

'I don't know, but this is not normal. He won't respond to me at all. I don't even think he can see me.'

'Do you think the worry has got to him?'

'No,' Trar answered after a pause. *'I think that something has got him trapped over a mind link. The only link he has is with Kalena so I would bet my tail feathers that whatever is happening to him has something to do with Kalena.'*

'Stay with him Trar. Tell me immediately there is any change in him.'

'Yes, Kral.' Tayme could feel Trar's rebuff in her response. Of course, she would stay with him, it was a stupid thing to ask.

Tayme was suddenly jostled from behind. He looked back in consternation to see a Pydarki rush pass him. Then something clipped his other shoulder and was surprised to see another Pydarki move ahead to push past the hulking Dymarki and Asnar. Within a few more steps, several more Pydarki rushed pass. Tayme stopped in his tracks and gazed in confusion at the sea of white suede that now abruptly flowed around him. The three ahead of him had also halted.

Where did all these people come from? There were now hundreds of Pydarki, both male and female, hurrying past them and all flowing in the same direction that they were going. The one thing that struck Tayme as he looked at all the faces moving about him was how shocked and alarmed they all looked. And how scared.

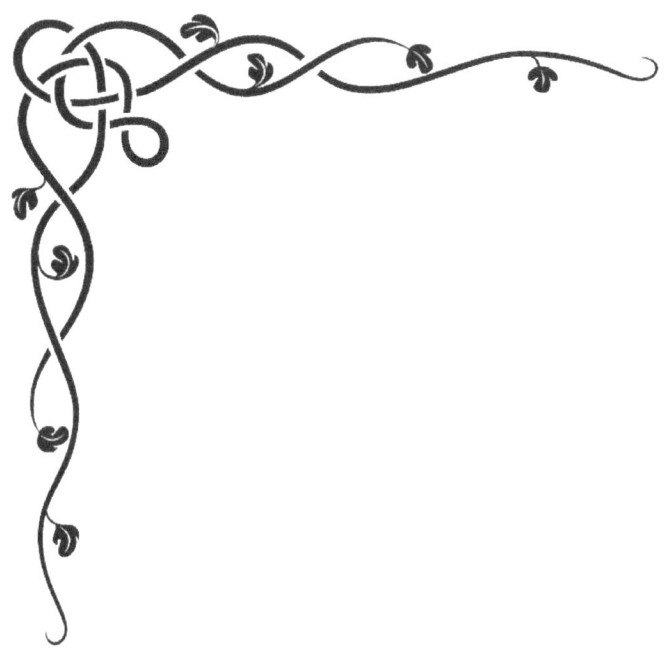

CHAPTER NINE

The humming in her head stopped as soon as Dearen's first step took her past the door, though the vibration from her Krytal Crystal still resonated through her skull. The floor had changed as she crossed the threshold from the worked stone flags of the outer corridor to a glassy material that felt cooler and smoother through the soles of her boots. In the arc of reflected light from the gemmed eyes of the Black Bisons on the doors, the rose colored floor reminded Dearen of the look of the dessert jellies that she had seen on the Freeman Officers tables at Darkon.

The vibration against her skull from behind her ear began to quicken, compelling her to take the final step to put her fully inside the hall. As soon as Dearen's foot hit the floor, a pulse of light rippled out from it across the crystal floor of the hall and then flowed up the rose pink walls to disappear into the ceiling. An answering bright, rosy glow streamed back down the walls lighting up the crystal walls as it ran back towards Dearen. As if activated by the light, the humming started up again, this time stronger and more melodic.

Behind her ear, Dearen felt an answering hum. It was a joyous music that sounded loud to her ear and the hall echoed the rhythm back to her. Dearen could feel its vibration from the floor through the soles of the feet. Where was the humming coming from? There was no one else that she could see in this room. Deep inside she began to feel afraid. This was way beyond her ken. As soon as these thoughts materialized, a feeling of peace and belonging flowed out from her Krytal and seeped through to the rest of her body.

A cry of surprise echoed through her mind, pulling her away from the tranquility that she was suddenly feeling. It was Adhamh, and through his link, Dearen heard the same hum she could hear coming from her own Krytal crystal. For a moment, her sight was disjointed, as if she was seeing through both Adhamh's and her own eyes at once. Trar's worried face, red feathers fluffed up and agitated, the rose hall around her, shining and sparkling as light reflected from the surrounding crystal.

Dearen staggered a few steps further in and then slowly sunk to her knees, both hands tightly clutching her head as if that could keep the sound of the crystal out of her mind. The humming did not sound threatening, but welcoming, as if she was a long lost daughter coming home after many years away. And that scared Dearen more than anything else she had faced before.

'Adhamh…what is…happening to us?'

'I…do not know…something to do…with our Krytal crystals.'

'It's this hall…the crystal…it's like

meeting…Sethi'de'hasma all over again.'

Dearen shuddered as she heard the memory of Sethi's sibilant whisper seep into her thoughts. '*…Now I have you my little mouse…*' Along with the voice came the memory of crimson feathers and the smell of death and decay.

'Not the same…this feels…benevolent…joyous…' Adhamh's voice grew stronger as he spoke and that strength flowed through the link to Dearen, chasing away the demons of her past.

"Adhamh!" Dearen cried out, and she threw back her head as her voice echoed around the Hall, quickly gaining in strength as it was amplified by the crystal. Dearen thought she heard an answering cry from the Hatar, but with all the noise around her wasn't sure.

Dearen kept her head back, her eyes closed tight against the rosy light around her, but closing out the external Hall made her realize that there was something inside her working internally.

The vibration had turned to a sharp tingling akin to the pins and needles you get in your foot when you keep it immobile for a period of time before you go to move it. The tingling felt like little ants swarming and wriggling just under her skin and the feeling fanned out from the spot just behind her ear and flowed out and over every part of her body until it turned back and stopped at the nape of her neck.

And then the tingling vanished.

'Kalena, Adhamhma'al'mearan. I know you can both hear me. Do not be afraid, I will not hurt you.'

The strange voice was strong in her mind and startled Dearen because of its clarity. It was then that she realized that the humming had stopped. She pulled her hands hesitantly from her ears and opened her eyes. She was still alone in the Hall. The crystal around her still produced the rose colored light and now that she was really looking, Dearen saw that what she took for blocks of crystal along the walls were in fact boxed shelves. And magically suspended in each box was a small colored piece of crystal that pulsed with its own inner light. Some of the boxes remained dark as if waiting for the light to come and fill it.

'Who are you?' She heard Adhamh ask.

'My name is Haylith and I welcome you both to my home.' The voice fluted again through her mind, reminding Dearen of the colors and

smells of spring and sunshine. From the walls around her came an answering chorus of welcomes. Dearen shifted in her crouch, kneeling on the hard crystal floor was beginning to feel a little painful.

'Where are you Haylith? Are you hiding from me?' Dearen asked as she continued to scan the hall for any signs of movement.

'Kalena, the Krytal...' Adhamh's voice whispered through her mind as the realization dawned on him. Dearen touched a hand to the scar behind her ear.

'Yes, Adhamh. I am in the Crystal matrix of both your Krytal crystals. The pair was once whole and when they were split to be given to both of you, so was I.'

'So...you're sentient? A living crystal?' Dearen asked in confusion.

'Not at first. I was once a living, breathing creature just like you. But times change and we must do as needs must.'

'I would not have thought that was possible,' Adhamh said, *'What were you before you entered the crystal? And how long have you been there?'*

Adhamh's question was met with a tinkling laugh. *'I have been in the crystal as best I can tell for over a millennium. I was the leader of my people. A free thinker and a philosopher. I was also a powerful Astromancer and pyromancer. My people owned the skies and made our homes in the mountains. I was what both your people would term, a dragon.'*

"A Dragon!" Dearen cried out in disbelief. "Dragons are just a tale parents tell to their children to make them behave.

'And yet we did exist. I know you heard the legend of the Black Bison. The man who escorted you here told you of it. Though his telling was simplistic, it did tell you that we and the bison disappeared at the same moment. Some of my people moved on to other lands while the oldest of us elected to go early to the memory vault so that our knowledge will not be lost to eternity.'

Dearen frowned. *'Do all Krytal crystals given to the Hatar Kalar contain the souls of dragons?'*

'No. The crystals that the people took from this hall before were empty of souls. The people here have been afraid of what might happen if an activated Krytal was used in a living host.'

'If they were afraid, why are you with

us?' Adhamh asked. Dearen could virtually hear his hunger for dragon knowledge bubble through their link. She tried not to smile. Adhamh loved history.

'That I cannot tell you. I and my people were to be released from our crystal matrix when my brethren return from across the seas and this land was well enough to support us. The fact that I have been used like this may not bode well for either of us. My son is not going to like this.'

'Why have you not shown yourself to us sooner?' Dearen asked as she pulled herself to her feet. The hard floor did hurt her knees.

'I couldn't before now, though you have had access to some of my available magic. I am only able to talk to you now because I can use the power stored in the crystal of this Hall and in the

mountain below us.'

'This is too unbelievable...'

Noise from the Hall entrance drew Dearen's attention and as she turned she saw hundreds of Pydarki gathered in the corridor beyond.

'Adhamh....'

'DEAREN!'

Hauga's voice suddenly blasted through her mind and Dearen shook her head to clear the last of the sound from her head.

"Hauga!" she called aloud and felt a flush of relief when she saw two Dymarki push their way through the crowd followed by Tayme. Then she caught sight of Asnar which bought some of her gall quickly to the rise.

"Kalena! You're alright. We were afraid that something had hap-" Tayme abruptly stopped mid-sentence and his feet followed suit. Raga and Hauga stood next to him and were both snarling in surprise.

"What's the matter?" Dearen took a step forward and then looked back over her shoulder to see if something had appeared behind her.

"Your hair…." Tayme started but the shock stifled his tongue.

'And your eyes… they are black.' Hauga finished for him.

Dearen quickly ran her hands through her hair but could not feel anything different. She took a handful and held it up to look at it. Her hair was still black, but now it also has streaks of blue running through it. Blue the same color as Adhmah's under belly. What had happened to her hair? What did that tingling do to her?

'Haylith-'

'Dearen, we can talk about this at length at a later time,' Adhamh's voice cut in.

'Yes, we might not be safe until we find out why I was used like this and why you were both chosen to hold my spirit.' Haylith quickly said.

'Very well.'

"My hair and eyes are fine. I think we all need to leave this place. And leave it NOW!"

Dearen did not wait for a response and just walked back past them to the door. The large crowd around the doorway parted silently for her and as she passed by they all bowed low to her.

'Dearen....' Hauga's tenuous mental voice whispered into her thoughts.

She stopped and turned on her heel to look at them. The four had followed her and were only a few feet behind her.

"Whatever it is can wait. We have some Northerner's to meet and we are going to leave as soon as we are packed. I've had my fill of this place and its secrets."

To Be Continued in

Part 11

The Mark of Fate

Thank you so much for reading and I hope to see you again.

Thank you for reading my book. If you enjoyed it, won't you please take a moment to leave me a review?

THE KALARTHRI
The Way to Freedom, Book One

"This Hatar Kalar has more natural Talent than any Second Born found in the Empire."

Every ten years the Imperium Provosts travel the provinces of the Great Suene Empire and take every second born child as the property of the Emperor. His Due for their continued protection.

Kalena, taken from her family and friends finds herself alone and scared in the imperial Stronghold of Darkon. And when she cries out to the darkness for help, Kalena is shocked when it answers her back.

If you found out that you were different from everyone else, what would you do?

HOWLING VENGEANCE
John McCall Mysteries, Book One

John McCall just wanted to get a surprise for his men. Instead he got a disemboweled body.

A man is arrested for the murder but McCall is sure that they have the wrong person.

And when McCall starts digging around for the truth, he unearths a whole lot more than he bargained for.

Howling Vengeance. A supernatural mystery in the Old West.

Available now at your favorite Online Bookseller

THE ENCLAVE
The Verge, Book One

Katherine Kirk lived only for vengeance.

Vengeance against the man who destroyed her home, her family and her life.

Sent on a babysitting mission to Junter 3, RAN officer Katherine Kirk, finds herself quickly embroiled in the politics between the New Holland Government and the Val Myran refugees claiming asylum.

After an Alliance attack Kirk and her team hunt the enemy down and discover that they have finally found the lair of the man they have been searching for…

And the captive who has been waiting patiently for rescue.

"What would you do to the man who destroyed every important person in your life?"

Winter's Magic

Book One of The Order

Kaitlyn Winter is biting at the bit to become an active agent for the Restricted Practitioners Unit. And on her first day in the job she is thrown into a virtual s**t storm (to put it nicely).

First, she gets targeted for Assassination by The Sharda's top assassin

Second, her Werewolf best friend decides that her being '*Straight*' means she can't protect herself and places her in protective custody

Third, the love of her life still won't notice her existence and the Tempus Mage who's set to keep an eye on her is infuriatingly attractive….

You can find out more information and sign up for Hayley's monthly newsletter on her website
http://www.hmclarkeauthor.com/

Proven
Book one of The Blackwatch Chronicles

Something is rotten in the city of Brookhaven. And it is up to the Blackwatch to root it out.

All Ryn Weaver ever wanted was to be a warrior. To protect others unable to protect themselves. But on her Proving to join the prestigious Blackwatch Order she finds herself accidentally Paired with Dagan Drake, a Tribunal Mage. Theirs is a reluctant partnership. Given no choice in the matter, Ryn must now work with Dagan to complete his mission to capture a traitor to the realm.

With rogue mages and brutish blades coming at her from every turn, will Ryn be able to gain the respect of her new partner and prove herself worthy of her blade? Or will Ryn and her Order fall to the machinations of the evil set against them?

Proven is the first installment in a new epic fantasy romance series. If you like electrifying action, rich characters, and magical battles, then you'll love H.M. Clarke's series starter

ABOUT THE AUTHOR

In a former life, H M Clarke has been a Console Operator, an ICT Project Manager, Public Servant, Paper Shuffler and an Accountant (the last being the most exciting.)

She attended Flinders University in Adelaide, South Australia, where she studied for a Bachelor of Science (Chem), and also picked up a Diploma in Project Management while working for the South Australian Department of Justice.

In her spare time, she likes to lay on the couch and watch TV, garden, draw, read, and tell ALL her family what wonderful human beings they are.

She keeps threatening to go out and get a real job (Cheesecake Test Taster sounds good) and intends to retire somewhere warm and dry – like the middle of the Simpson Desert. For the time being however, she lives in Ohio and dreams about being warm…

You can find out more information and sign up for Hayley's monthly newsletter on her website –
http://hmclarkeauthor.com
http://eepurl.com/SPy61

Or catch her on Twitter - **@hmclarkeauthor**

Made in the USA
Las Vegas, NV
28 February 2021